First North American edition published
in 2013 by Boxer Books Limited.
www.boxerbooks.com
Boxer® is a registered trademark of Boxer Books Limited

Text copyright © 2013 Boxer Books Limited.
Illustrations copyright © 2008 Beverlie Manson
The right of Beverlie Manson to be identified
as the illustrator of this work has been asserted by her in accordance
with the Copyright, Designs and Patents Act, 1988.

ISBN 978-1-907967-57-3

1 3 5 7 9 10 8 6 4 2

Printed in China

All of our papers are sourced from managed
forests and renewable resources.

SECRET
Diaries
FAIRIES

ILLUSTRATED BY
BEVERLIE MANSON

BOXER BOOKS

FAIRIES' FAVORITE THINGS

In our secret diaries we keep all our private thoughts and favorite memories. Every fairy has a special place to treasure things that are important to them. Shhh, keep it secret.

Some favorite fairy things:

Spring

Unicorns

Secrets

Honey

MY FAVORITE THINGS

MY NAME Shawna

MY AGE 8

MY FAVORITE THINGS Cats icecream

HERE IS A PHOTO
OF ME AGED

8

YEARS

FAIRIES' NEW YEAR'S RESOLUTIONS

Dear Diary,

Today is January 1st

and we made resolutions.

    I will always listen.

    I will take good care

    of the baby unicorn.

I will always help

the little ones.

    I will share with others.

What are your New Year's Resolutions?

listen to my mother and father better

9

JANUARY

Today, I helped Amey look
after the fairy babies as
they played.

JANUARY

Which of your New Year's
Resolutions have you kept?

JANUARY

Dear Diary,

Frost upon the berries is simply the prettiest thing in January. What do you love about January?

JANUARY

Why don't you leave out
some tasty treats for the
winter birds in your garden.
Make a note of which birds
visit to enjoy the feast.

JANUARY

January evenings are
dark and long. I make
paper lanterns. What
do you do?

FEBRUARY

Dear Diary,

We're planning a Valentine's Day Party for tomorrow night. We'll all dress up. We'll watch the Fairy Valentine's Parade. Then we'll sit in the big tree and eat red berry hearts with pomegranate juice.

Shhhh! I know who will give me a Valentine, but who will get one from me? Check back tomorrow to learn the secret.

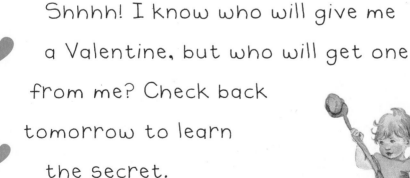

♥ FEBRUARY ♥

MY SECRET ADMIRERS

Shhh. Don't tell. I sent a Valentine to
Oren. And Digby sent one to me!

Will you be sending a Valentine?
Who to?

VALENTINE

FEBRUARY

Dear Diary,
   The nights are
   still cold and
   frosty. Luckily
   Cassia is around
   to keep us all
   warm with a
   flicker from her
beautiful wings.

FEBRUARY

What are your favorite ways to warm up on cold nights? Hot chocolate and marshmallows, fleecy blankets and snug hats? Write a few of them here:

FEBRUARY

Today I am very excited. Elvin and I are going to learn how to make fairy light. Fairy light is very special as it never goes out and shines more brightly the darker it is, when you need it the most.

FEBRUARY

Winter is nearly over.
Time to make plans for
the spring. What plans
have you made?

SPRING

MARCH

Hooray. Spring has sprung! The sunshine has come out at last and we can see the first flowers unfolding their delicate petals to say hello.

Lorelle and I are going on a special trip to tiptoe through the bluebells. Only fairies can do this as each bluebell is specially protected by fairy dust and we have the tiniest teeniest feet.

MARCH

Try drawing some flowers that
you have seen:

MARCH

Can you go and visit
some bluebell woods?
Imagine how many
fairies there are dancing
among the flowers
– so tiny you can't
see them. You must
tread very carefully.

MARCH

Dear Diary,

Today, I have seen five newborn chicks, and danced with the butterflies. Time for some honey I think. It's thirsty work tending to all these new animals.

MARCH

Dear Diary,

Today, I promised to help Cecilia color some of the late spring flowers. Quinn was watching us closely.

He is the florist for the Fairy Queen and says he needs to watch the flowers. But I think secretly he was watching Cecilia!

MARCH

Are you ready for Easter? Who will you give an Easter egg to?

EASTER

APRIL

Dear Diary,

Ella found the first colored
egg at the Easter Egg Hunt.
She wouldn't let anyone else
see it until the hunt was over.

Celeste and Annabelle
found one and they
shared it with everyone.

Esme was too busy eating
cherries to look for eggs.
She looked like she was
wearing red lipstick! She's
too young for lipstick!

APRIL

Did you have an Easter Egg Hunt
this Easter? Did you paint any eggs?
Tell us all about your Easter:

APRIL

April showers are here again.
Luckily the Enchanted Bells
and Fairy Ferns make good
fairy umbrellas.

Try designing your own giant flower hat – right here!

APRIL

Dear Diary,

This morning the nightingale woke me up with her singing. She has the most beautiful voice. I wish I could sing like her.

What songs do you know?

APRIL

Ruby was not too happy about
being awakened. She spent all day
yesterday entertaining Stone with
magic tricks and was very tired!
So she was a little grumpy.

Can you remember
your dreams?

MAY

Today, I made a daisy chain. Can you make one too? Give it to a special friend to show her how much you care.

MAY

What do you love most
about your friends?

MAY

Christabelle has
just been crowned
Spring Fairy Queen.
She's beautiful.

Every fairy gets to present her with a
gift. Hunter is giving her a baby unicorn,
and I am going to give her a bouquet of
pink fairy blossoms.

MAY

Dear Diary,

The squirrel family just got bigger.
Mrs. S. has had three baby kittens.
They are very sweet, but she can't
get them to sleep, so Thistle has
been singing them lullabies. He might
have to learn a new one soon!

42

MAY

What are your favorite songs?

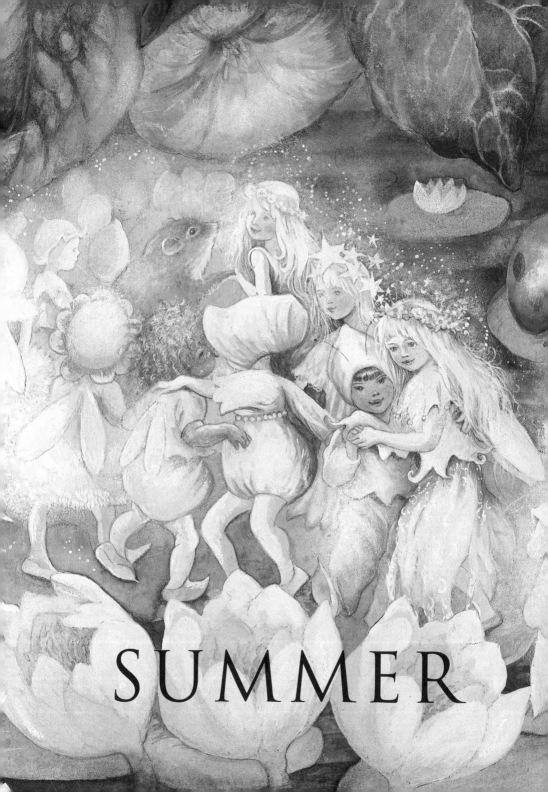

SUMMER

JUNE

Dear Diary,

Today, Elvin and I were tested on what we learned in February! We had to make fifty fairy lanterns for the summer procession tonight. I do hope they shine perfectly all night. What would happen if one of them went out?

46

JUNE

JUNE

Dear Diary,

Today, Bethany is teaching Apple
how to dance. She will teach us
all the fairy waltz in time for the
Summer Ball.

JUNE

Thiske and Daisy are
perfect together.
They always get the
steps right.

I might need a
little fairy dust
to help me!
One, two, three,
one, two, three ...

JUNE

Dear Diary,

Exciting news! I've just heard that the ladybug, lacewing, frog, and butterfly will be the band for this year's Summer Ball. They have a new band name: Tooty Flutey. They play the most brilliant music.

JUNE

Who would you most like to dance with?

JULY

Dear Diary,

I'm sorry it took me so long
to write. The Summer Ball was
a huge success. Bethany led the
dancing with Lord Squirrel.

Jasmine and Lily were enchanted.
They think Bethany is the best
dancer. Summer is our
favorite season. We
have so much to do!

JULY

Dear Diary,

Today, Jasmine and I were trying
to decide if we prefer sunlight or
moonlight, swans or butterfly boats.

Dancing or singing, flowers or leaves.
We can't choose. We love everything
about summer. What do you love most?

AUGUST

Dear Diary,

Long summer nights are perfect for
camping out under the stars and
dancing all night long.

AUGUST

What are your favorite
summer activities?

AUGUST

Today, I have mostly been drawing. The moonlight on the water last night was so beautiful I wanted to keep it forever and capture it in my diary.

Ladybug

Here is my picture of a ladybug.

AUGUST

Why don't you draw something that you think captures all the fun of summer:

AUGUST

I found this lovely poem in a book.
I really like it. It is by a lady named
Rose Amy Fyleman. It goes like this:
"Dance, little friend,
little friend breeze,
Low among the hedgerows,
high among the trees."

Do you know any poems?

AUGUST

What were the most wonderful things you saw this summer?

SEPTEMBER

Dear Diary,

Summer has come to an end.
It was splendid! Now Fall
is here, it's back to fairy
lessons – flying, singing,
folklore, care for others,
and cooking with all the Fall
forest fruit.

SEPTEMBER

Things to remember for first
day at school:

SEPTEMBER

Dear Diary,

I love the Fall colors:
glimmering gold, burnt
orange, and russet reds.
And there is so much
fairy dust everywhere.
It's a fairy secret that
fairy dust helps change
all the colors from the
bright summer greens
to the fiery Fall reds, so
smoothly you can't see it
with your eyes.

SEPTEMBER

Chrystal and Tomkin are fascinated by fairy dust. Tomkin tried to blow it ... but it went up his nose and he sneezed. I couldn't stop giggling.

SEPTEMBER

Dear Diary,

Today is Harvest Festival. We have so many things to say thank you for – berries, nuts, fruits, seeds, and mushrooms. It takes a special fairy to know which foods are safe to eat – the animals all go to Orial for help.

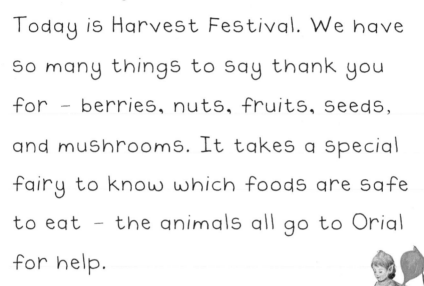

I'll try to sit next to Orial. I'm sure he will know all the answers to the Harvest Quiz.

FALL

OCTOBER

Harvest Quiz:

What do squirrels
like best to eat?

Which berries have
the best colors?

Which currants make
the best fairy jelly?

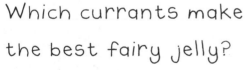

OCTOBER

Toadstools and mushrooms
make great fairy seats.

Never eat toadstools,
mushrooms, or berries
that you find.
They could be poison.

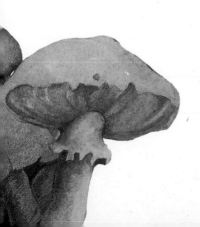 

OCTOBER

Dear Diary,

Today was a very exciting day. Azora,
Queen of the Elves, came to visit
on Glade, her unicorn. She crowned
Clementine the Fall Fairy Queen.

OCTOBER

It was funny because Clementine was still asleep and Azora had to wake her! Poor Clem. She blushed! But the whole day was magical.

OCTOBER

Bonnie has made a beautiful bonnet to celebrate Fall. I'm going to try and make a hat of my own. Maybe I could make one out of an acorn?

OCTOBER

Can you draw a picture of a fairy hat
you would love to wear?

NOVEMBER

Dear Diary,

I've found another wonderful

poem by Rose Amy Fyleman.

Here is a bit of it:

"A fairy went a marketing

She bought a

winter gown

All stitched

about with

gossamer

And lined with

thistledown."

NOVEMBER

Do you have a favorite winter dress?
Please draw a picture of it here:

NOVEMBER

Dear Diary,

Today, we had flying
classes with Faylin.
Saira was my partner.
We were supposed to be
improving, so our flights are less
bumpy. But we got distracted
by a fairy dust shower
and flew into the
Winter Fairy Bells!
Oops.

NOVEMBER

If you had fairy wings, what would
yours look like?

NOVEMBER

Dear Diary,

It is Thanksgiving, but

I'm already looking forward

to Christmas

and the Midwinter Feast.

Eldon and Myrtle

will sit nearby so

we can all share

our secret wishes.

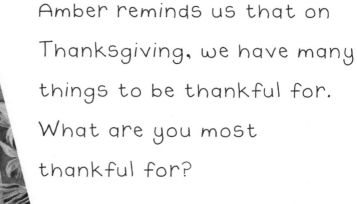

Amber reminds us that on

Thanksgiving, we have many

things to be thankful for.

What are you most

thankful for?

NOVEMBER

What would you like to eat at a
Midwinter Feast?

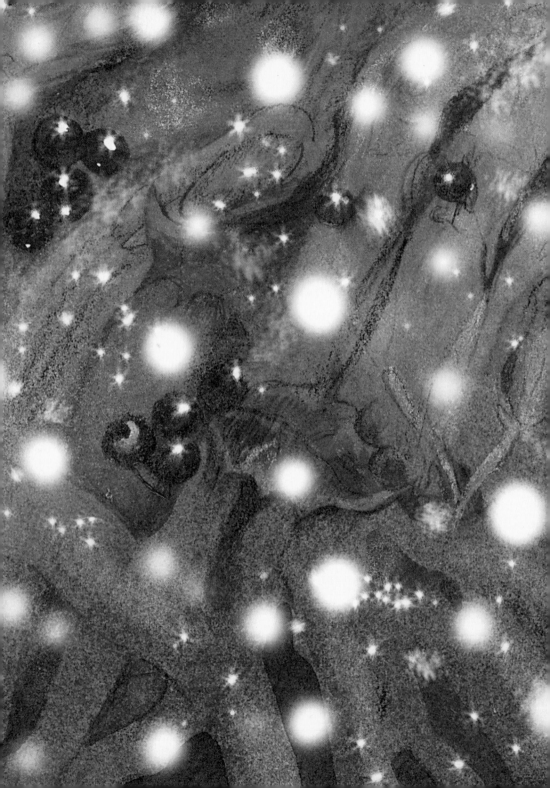

WINTER

DECEMBER

Dear Diary,

It's December at last and our Midwinter Feast is getting closer.

I can't wait to sit around the candles in the cold darkness and listen to all the fairy stories.

DECEMBER

Do you have a favorite story
for a cold winter's night?

DECEMBER

Dear Diary,
I think I am most
excited about
seeing Noelle.
She is so pretty
and has the
most fantastic
cloak made out
of frosty beads
and a necklace
made of snowflakes.
I would love
a necklace like that.

DECEMBER

Is this a good time to write your
Christmas list and send it to Santa?

CHRISTMAS

CHRISTMAS

Dear Diary,

Noelle was here! And the feast was amazing. The table was laid with every winter berry and nut you could possibly imagine. The hall was decorated with mistletoe and garland.

CHRISTMAS

It was Corbin's first Christmas so Joy had to keep a special eye on him. He was so excited he couldn't sit still! And I had to stop Twinkle from climbing on the table!

NEXT YEAR

Here are my fairy resolutions for next
year. Some are the same as last year!

I will always be kind.

I will always listen.

I will get better at flying.

I will share my fairy dust.

I will look after the Robin Redbreast.

HAPPy NEW yEAR!

NEXT YEAR

What are your New year's Resolutions?